Meadow VOLE

Reva Cotter

Balboa Press books may be ordered through booksellers or by contacting:

Balboa Press
A Division of Hay House
1663 Liberty Drive
Bloomington, IN 47403
www.balboapress.com
1 (877) 407-4847

Because of the dynamic nature of the Internet, any web addresses or links contained in this book may have changed since publication and may no longer be valid. The views expressed in this work are solely those of the author and do not necessarily reflect the views of the publisher, and the publisher hereby disclaims any responsibility for them.

Any people depicted in stock imagery provided by Getty Images are models, and such images are being used for illustrative purposes only.
Certain stock imagery © Getty Images.

ISBN: 978-1-9822-3682-3 (sc)
ISBN: 978-1-9822-3681-6 (e)

Library of Congress Control Number: 2019916171

Print information available on the last page.

Balboa Press rev. date: 01/21/2020

Once there was a meadow vole that lived between Fresh Pond and Seneca Swamp. Each was so beautiful Meadow Vole could not decide which was more desirable, so she would meander back and forth between the two, loving each for what she considered nature's beautiful spaces of glory.

Although Meadow Vole lived alone in various holes
and sometimes under stonewalls, trees, bushes or
even houses, she had many island friends.
Her friendships were endless, expansive like the island's sky,
the moon, stars, sun, flowers, trees, and many creatures
like painted turtles, frogs, beetles, muskrats, red winged
black birds, ducks, eastern red bats, eastern bluebirds and
jays, great ibis, herons, dragonflies, butterflies, and bees
who bring their nectar to make Block Island honey.

Each morning Meadow Vole would welcome the day by watching the sunrise. First the color red would appear in the sky, and then orange followed by yellow, green, blue, purple and white. She likened it to a rainbow of sorts as the colors expanded throughout the sky and relished in its power.

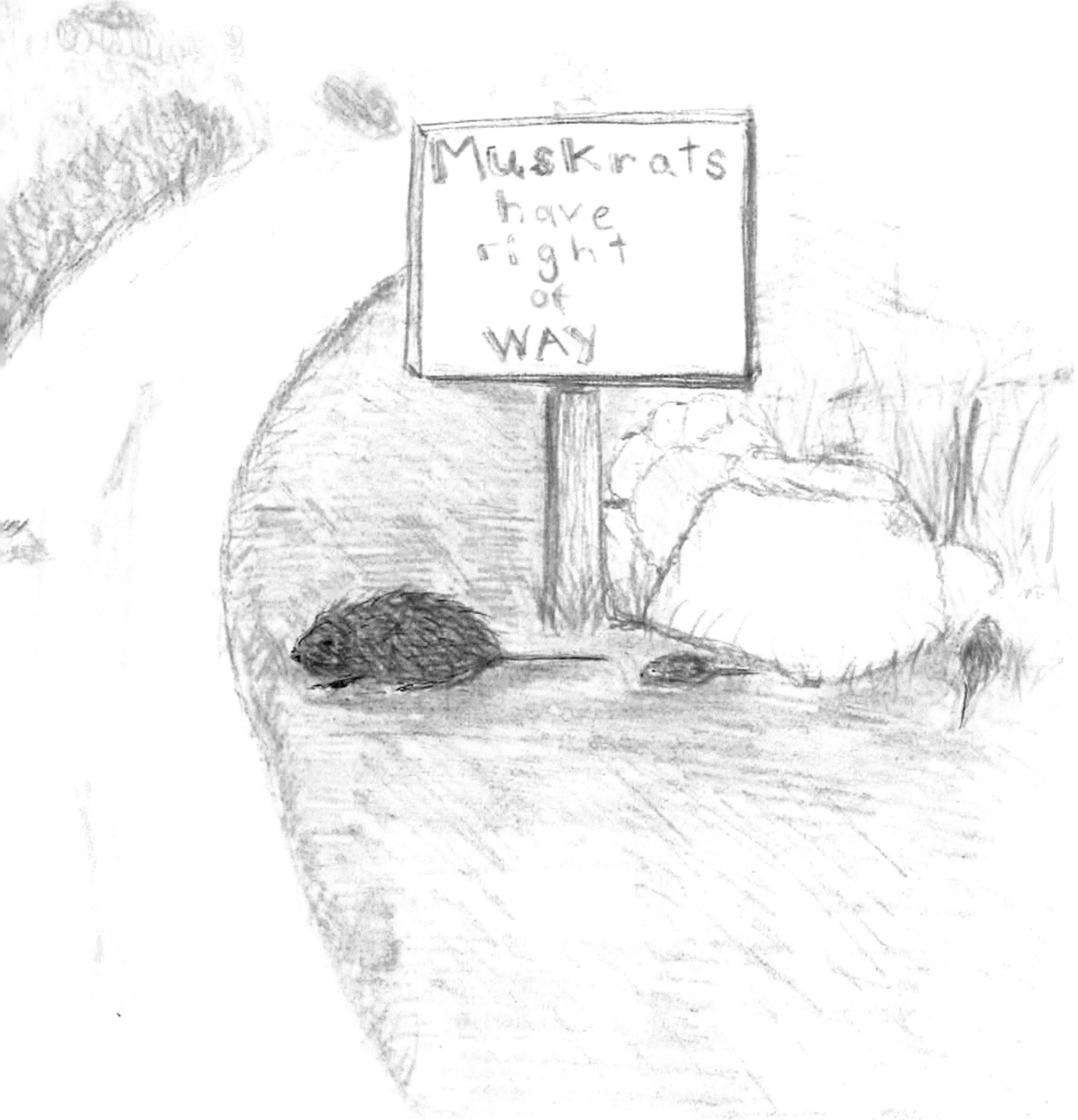
Muskrats
have
right
of
WAY

Meadow vole loved to swim and float in the pond and swamp although she would always have an eye out for a passing snake or snapping turtles. She would dry herself easily while snuggling in the grass and wonder about her upcoming day and if she might find a berry or mushroom to nibble.

Sometimes humans would appear in the houses between the waterways and she would watch them unload their belongings and animals, hop on their bikes or swim, row boats, paddle the raft, kayak or paddle board from place to place. She liked to see them be neighborly and visit each other as well, and knew to be careful while visiting dogs and cats were around.

Meadow Vole decided on this day she might make a new friend. So she strolled from her nest under a stonewall and greeted a baby muskrat sitting by some tall pond grass close to some lily pads. She could tell he was sad since there was no smile on his face; he was looking down and with a frown on his sweet face.

"Why the long face muskrat?" Inquired Meadow Vole.
"Hello, who are you?" Swamp Muskrat wondered aloud.
"I am Meadow Vole, I live between the pond and the
swamp, between here and there," she replied.

"I am feeling down about my favorite tree, it recently split apart after lightning struck one night, there are many beetles and a stump with branches and needles everywhere. It used to be my home," explained Swamp Muskrat.

"Oh my," empathized Meadow Vole, "that does appear to be sad at first. It sounds to me like the tree is actually decomposing. Do you mean disappearing into the ground?" Swamp Muskrat shook his head yes.

"The good news is that the tree is still giving life even as it seems to be disappearing into the ground. All those tree parts have many nutrients, which are like vitamins for the soil and other plants, like mushrooms and flowers and new trees will enjoy those gifts left behind." Meadow Vole was glad to contribute something positive to the conversation with her newfound friend and she was happy to be learning something too. Decomposing was a big word, and she thought about the time it would take, and if it would happen in her lifetime?

Swamp Muskrat pondered this new information as both little creatures noticed some much larger ones playing in rowboats and on a floating dock nearby. They could hear the kids playing a game.

Meadow Vole thought to herself, "this could not have been better timing" and much appreciated the help that had unknowingly arrived. "Let's join in the fun those kids are having Muskrat" Suggested Meadow Vole.

"What are they doing?" Swamp Muskrat curiously asked, as he was young and eager to learn new games. It was especially enticing because muskrats spend most of their lives in the water, building their nests and raising their families.

"Oh these kids do this all day long, it's a game they call, 'Ferry.' They go back and forth and back and forth between coves and rocks they have named after all the kids, and transport passengers from one dock, to rock, to the coves and back to the pond's beach, then on to the next, some might call it island hopping!" described Meadow Vole nonchalantly.

"How do we join in?" Swamp Muskrat was getting excited to play!
"Easily, let's pull a few feathers and leaves together on top
of this old tree branch, we should thank the tree that has
become a float over time as it decomposes, for our boat seats,
and that should be sufficient to keep our ferry afloat."

So all day long the kids played in the pond and Meadow Vole and Swamp Muskrat did as well, co-existing in a playful and peaceful manner, the way Mother Nature intended for all creatures to get along.

Later that evening as the kids went home to their beds in the houses between the pond and the swamp, Meadow Vole and Swamp Muskrat settled into their new home by the stone wall, tree stump and old branches. They had fixed it up with dry feathers, leaves, and reed grass for warmth and coverage. Mushrooms were already sprouting to provide breakfast for them in the morning, as they would enjoy another sunrise, this time together. Little did they know they would remain friends until the end of their lifetime and that their friends and families would continue on this beautiful friendship of lake, land, and sky.

For now, it had been another lovely day in the spaces between here and there on their Block Island home where the opportunity to make a friend had changed their lives forever.

Latitude: 41°10' 24.7634"
Longitude: -71° 35' 6.0673"

Giovanni de Verrazzano was the
first European to note Block Island's
existence in 1524. Block Island
was named after Adrion Block,
the Dutch navigator who
rediscovered the island in
1614.

BLOCK ISLAND is:
7 miles long
and
3 miles wide
There are 2 types of
snakes

Three types of turtles

three species of
amphibians

many avian
species

and bats
spend their
lifecycles
on
and
near the
Island.

www.blockisland.com

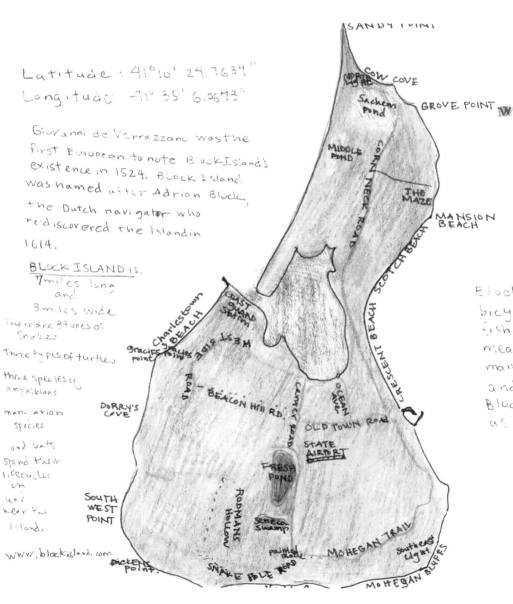

SANDY POINT

COW COVE

NORTH LIGHT

Sachem Pond

GROVE POINT

MIDDLE POND

CORN NECK ROAD

THE MAZE

MANSION BEACH

SCOTCH BEACH

CRESCENT BEACH

CHARLESTOWN BEACH

COAST GUARD STATION

WEST SIDE ROAD

Gracies Bales Point

DORRY'S COVE

BEACON HILL RD.

OCEAN AVE.

OLD TOWN ROAD

CONNER ROAD

STATE AIRPORT

FRESH POND

SOUTH WEST POINT

RODMANS HELLOW

SENECA SWAMP

MOHEGAN TRAIL

Southeast Light

DICKENS POINT

Pointed Rock

SNAKE HOLE ROAD

MOHEGAN BLUFFS

N

NW 330 | 30 NE
300 | 60
W 270 | 90 E
240 | 120
SW 210 | 150 SE
180
S

Block Island is known for
bicycling, hiking, sailing,
fishing, beaches, and the
meadow vole, muskrat, and
many other animals, plants,
and two historic lighthouses.
Block Island is also known
as New Shoreham.

Printed in the United States
By Bookmasters